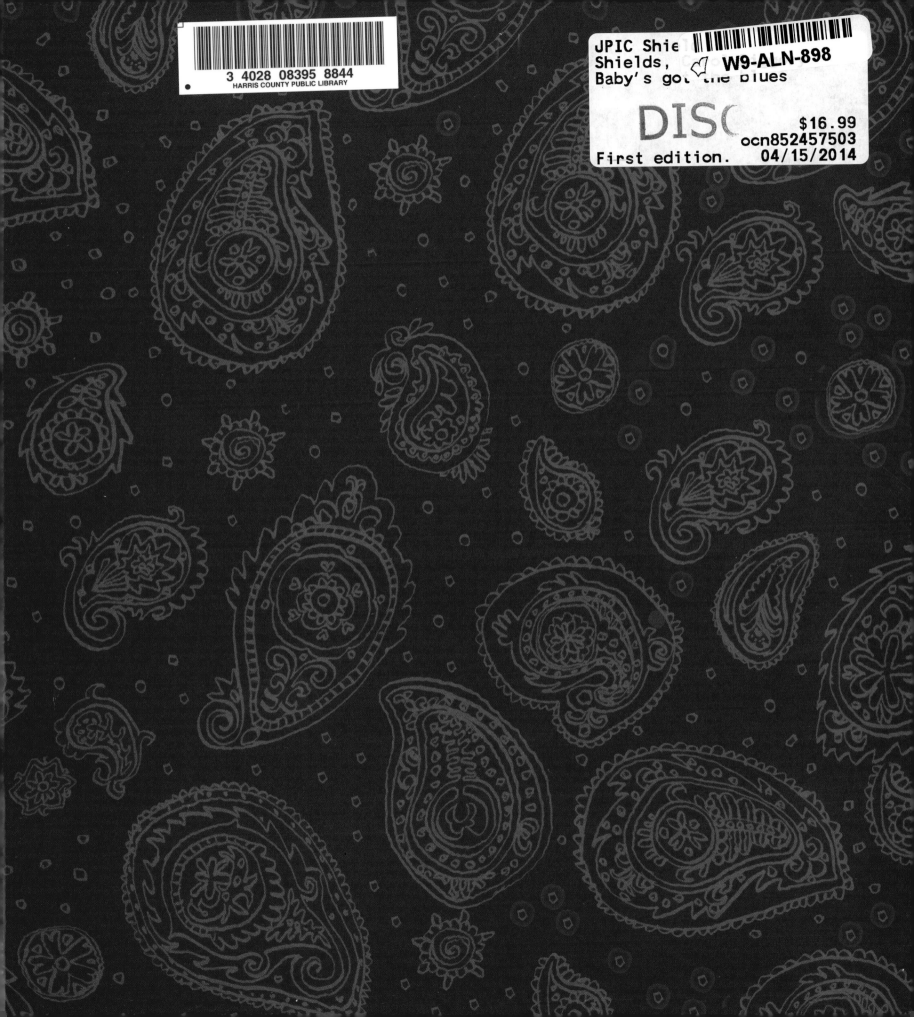

For Cal, with all Nana's love
C. D. S.

For Peter Tobia, "Grandad"
L. T.

Text copyright © 2014 by Carol Diggory Shields
Illustrations copyright © 2014 by Lauren Tobia

First edition 2014

Library of Congress Catalog Card Number 2013943085
ISBN 978-0-7636-3260-1

13 14 15 16 17 18 TLF 10 9 8 7 6 5 4 3 2 1

Printed in Dongguan, Guangdong, China

This book was typeset in Dodson.
The illustrations were done in ink and pencil
and assembled digitally.

Candlewick Press
99 Dover Street
Somerville, Massachusetts 02144

visit us at www.candlewick.com

BABY'S GOT THE BLUES

Carol Diggory Shields

illustrated by Lauren Tobia

CANDLEWICK PRESS

You think babies
have it easy?

Let me tell you, that's a lie.
Sometimes being a baby
Is enough to make you cry,
'Cause I'm a baby,
And I've got those baby blues.

B-A-B-Y, baby,

Got the poor little baby blues.

Woke up this morning soggy,
And that smell
    kept getting riper.
But I can't talk,
    no way to say,

"Won't somebody change my diaper?"

'Cause I'm a baby,
Got those baby stinkeroos.

B-A-B-Y,
baby,

Got those damp old baby blues.

I'd like to eat some pizza,
Macaroni, or beef stew,
But I haven't got a single tooth,

So I can't even chew.

I'm a baby,
And I never
get to choose.

B-A-B-Y,
baby,

I've got the
hungry baby blues.

I'm watching all the bigger kids—
They run and jump and race.
But every time I try to walk,

I fall flat on my face.

I'm a baby,
Can't even tie my shoes.

A B-A-B-Y,
baby,

With the goin'-nowhere
baby blues.

You say a little baby
Has no right to weep and wail,
But I'm doing time behind
these bars—

Is it a crib
or is it jail?

I'm a baby,
Paying my baby dues.

B-A-B-Y,
baby,

Got those locked-up
baby blues.

Sometimes I'm feeling low-down,
Snifflin', "Boo-hoo, boo-hoo-hoo."

Then someone scoops me up
With a "Kitchy-kitchy-koo!

B-A-B-Y, baby,

Don't you know
we all love you?"

And all those hugs and kisses
Make me lose those baby blues.

I'm a baby,
And I lost those low-down blues,
A B-A-B-Y, baby,

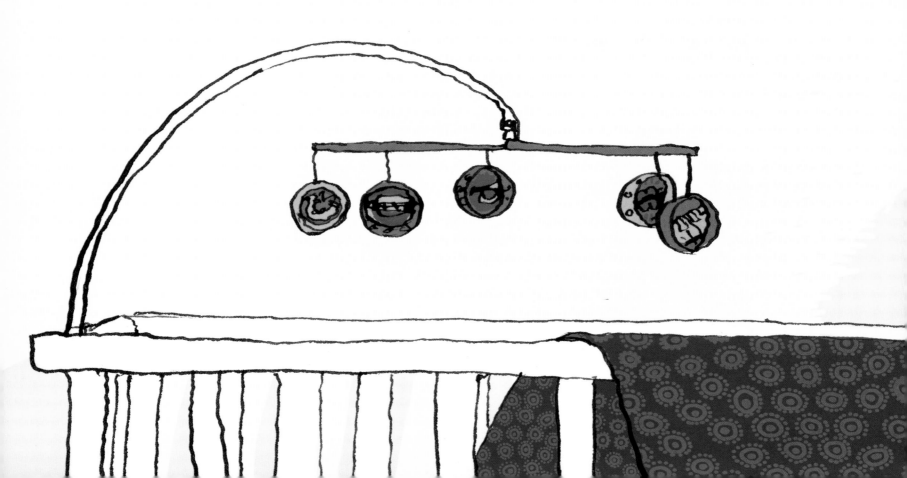

Cuddled up in I love yous.